THE GYPSIES' TALE

THE GYPSIES' TALE

by Ethel Pochocki · illustrated by Laura Kelly

SIMON & SCHUSTER BOOKS FOR YOUNG READERS
Published by Simon & Schuster
New York   London   Toronto   Sydney   Tokyo   Singapore

SIMON & SCHUSTER BOOKS FOR YOUNG READERS
Simon & Schuster, Rockefeller Center, 1230 Avenue of the Americas
New York, New York 10020. Text copyright © 1994 by Ethel Pochocki
Illustrations copyright © 1994 by Laura Kelly. All rights reserved including the
right of reproduction in whole or in part in any form. SIMON & SCHUSTER
BOOKS FOR YOUNG READERS is a trademark of Simon & Schuster.
Designed by David Neuhaus. The text for this book is set in 15 point Berkeley
Old Style. The illustrations were done in watercolor.

Manufactured in the United States of America
10 9 8 7 6 5 4 3 2 1

Library of Congress Cataloging-in-Publication Data
Pochocki, Ethel. The gypsies' tale / by Ethel Pochocki: illustrated by Laura
Kelly. p. cm. Summary: A gypsy couple's kindness to the birds outside
their cottage is repaid when their faithful old cherry tree begins to die.
[1. Cherry—Fiction.   2. Trees—Fiction.   3. Birds—Fiction.
4. Gypsies—Fiction.]   I. Kelly, Laura (Laura C.), ill.   II. Title.
PZ7.P7494Gy 1994 [E]—dc20 93-3320 CIP
ISBN: 0-671-79934-7

To Lorena with love
—E.P.

To Pat and Bill Farrell,
for their amazing enthusiasm
and friendship
—L.K.

Once upon a time a young gypsy and his wife grew tired of the traveling life and came to live in the deep wood. They cleared a spot of land near a spring that had bubbled and gushed before there was a wood, and built a cottage big enough and small enough for them to be happy in.

It had a thatched roof and pretty windows with pots of parsley on the sills and a root cellar for the turnips and beets they would grow in their garden. Brambles of wild blackberries ringed the cottage and kept back the forest; and alongside the house, near the kitchen window, grew a young cherry tree.

In the spring it danced in the wind like a young girl, shaking its white blossoms as if they were curls. When the gypsy and his wife watched from the kitchen window, they laughed to see such a thing; and the tree, like a true performer, bowed when they clapped their hands. And when they sat beneath it and the petals fell like April snow into their mugs of tea, they could hardly speak for the sudden beauty of it.

The cherry tree fed not only their spirits but their bodies as well. In summer they picked baskets and buckets of fruit, and each year the crop grew larger and the branches bowed more heavily with the tree's bounty.

The birds of the deep wood came and helped themselves to the fruit at the very top, where the gypsy and his wife could not reach.

"Let them have them," said the gypsy to his wife, who was a little put out at not getting every single cherry. "The birds are gypsies like we are. The earth is their mother, too, and shares her gifts with us all. Why do you ask for more work than you need?"

The woman knew he was right. So she forgot about the birds and started making the pies and tarts and jams to sell at the weekly market in the village. Here she also brought bunches of herbs and horseradish roots for colds and a salve for boils that she made from beeswax and pine resin and garlic.

Her husband, who could do a little of everything, came with her and spent the day shoeing horses and patching pots and pans for the women of the village. Sometimes he was paid in money, sometimes in bits of this and that. He refused nothing, for he saw possibility in every cracked piece of pottery, every broken bead, every length of tin or leather.

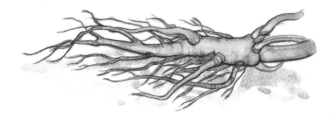

After market day they would come home tired but happy, eager to sit under the tree and exchange stories of how they used their wits. But first they would bathe in the wooden tub by the spring, washing themselves with oak leaves in the icy water, listening to the birds putting down their children for the night.

And so the years passed, and as you might expect, the gypsy and his wife and the tree grew older together. Their limbs stiffened, and they were less able to bend and dip with the playful wind.

The blossoms of the cherry tree were scanty now, and its bark was rough and peeling. Still, it did its best for the couple. It still gave enough fruit for a dozen pies and one batch of jam, which the wife saved for themselves.

Then a very hot, dry summer came upon the deep wood, when even the animals lay down under the pines and panted. They were too hot to play games or fight or dig holes. The spring no longer gushed but trickled to a whisper, and the gypsy and his wife could get only enough water to wash their faces and make their morning tea.

The poor cherry tree, thirsty as well, still loyally put forth its meager crop. It was not surprising that the birds began to eat the cherries, all of them, even those on the lower limbs. The gypsy's wife shouted and banged her pans to shoo them off.

"Do something about those birds!" she ordered her husband. "Look, they have eaten clear down to *our* cherries. They will leave us nothing." She began to sigh and cry loudly and wipe her nose on her apron. The gypsy put his hands over his ears and tried to think.

Finally, he went into the wood and in a little while brought back strands of young, wiry grapevine. He got out his box of odds and ends, and dumped the dishes and silverware and prisms and pipes onto the kitchen table.

The next morning he went out to the cherry tree and hung six wind chimes on it. The chimes clanged and clinked and rattled and rippled, making music that never before had been heard in the deep wood. And as the gypsy hoped, it frightened the birds from the tree, and so his wife was able to pick enough cherries for two pies, one to sell and one to eat.

In time the autumn winds blew on the tree like a trumpet, and all the leaves fell, and the chimes hung naked for all to see. The prisms and glass beads sparkled in the sun, and the string of old cups with violets painted on them clanged gently. The flattened spoons and forks rang like dinner bells, and the wind sang softly through the dangle of tin whistles.

The birds flying overhead saw all this and now knew they had nothing to fear. The curious things made music just as they did, but not as true or pure. They sat on the branches next to the chimes and twittered and caroled their bird song along with them. Even in winter's snow they came, the cardinal and blue jays and foolish nuthatches hanging upside down.

The gypsy's wife was touched as she watched them giving so freely of their song, expecting nothing in return.

"We must get some suet when we go to the village," she said. "The birds are hungry."

"I do not understand you, woman." The gypsy sighed, shaking his head. "First you tell me to get rid of the birds. Now you want me to feed them."

"There is nothing wrong with feeding birds in winter. They can't eat the cherries then," she said.

"You're absolutely right," said the gypsy, knowing he would never get the better of his wife.

And they hung the suet, which the wife had stuffed with millet and thistle seeds and cranberries, next to each of the wind chimes. The birds flocked to the tree, in such numbers you would think they were its blossoms, and put on a splendid show of song and aerial tricks, as if to say thank-you.

When spring came, the tree bore only five cherries, which the couple ate mournfully on a summer's evening.

The years passed, the gypsy couple grew older, and the cherry tree gave no more fruit. But the couple never forgot the tree's generosity of its youth.

One summer evening, the birds gathered together and chirped long and intently, as if conferring. The next morning they congregated beneath the gypsies' window, making such a commotion they woke the old couple.

Startled, the gypsy and his wife hurried outside and watched the chattering birds, time and again flying off and then returning. A cardinal flew directly to the woman's feet and tugged on her nightgown with his beak.

"I think they want us to follow them," said the husband.
His wife agreed. Quickly they changed their clothes, and
followed the birds, pushing past the bramble thickets, the
wooden tub, and the gushing-again spring; past the fairy
rings and brooding pines and vines of wild grape—so thick
you could swing on them—deeper and deeper into the wood
where they had never gone before.

Finally, they came out of the dark wood and climbed a small hill into a clearing. What a sight awaited them! Dancing in the sun was a grove of young cherry trees, their satiny barks glinting, the ripe, crimson cherries dropping in clumps to the ground.

"Ohhhhhhhhh," said the gypsy's wife. "I have never seen such cherries! Where did they come from? How long have they been here?"

The cardinal, already busy in the tree, answered her question by plucking a cherry and dropping it to the ground. Then he dropped another, and another, until the cherries lay in a row as neat and orderly as the trees themselves. The gypsies watched with their wise eyes, and understood everything.

And so the gypsy and his wife picked cherries until they ran out of containers in which to carry them. The woman filled her apron until it overflowed, and the gypsy did the same with his shirt and hat. They would have to come again, for there were enough cherries left for at least one hundred pies.

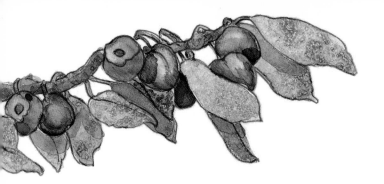

That night, by the light of the waxing moon, the gypsy's wife planted a cherry pit alongside the dying old tree, so that in a few springs she could once again watch the merry dance of the cherry tree from her kitchen window.